THE GLASS ANGELS

G*The*LASS ANGELS

Susan Hill

Illustrated by Valerie Littlewood

LONG BARN BOOKS

PUBLISHED BY
LONG BARN BOOKS

Ebrington Gloucestershire GL55 6NW

First published 1991
Copyright © Susan Hill 2009

Set in Garamond

Printed and bound by 1010 Printing International Ltd.

ISBN: 978-1-902421-28-5

CHAPTER ONE

'Wait,' said Tilly, 'wait. You're walking too fast. But just as she spoke they came around the corner onto the sea front and her voice was caught up on the whirl of the wind and drowned in the boom of the sea below. So her mother didn't hear her.

It was raining too, hard, cold rain like pins on their faces. For once, Tilly was quite glad that her mackintosh had been somebody else's and so was too big. It came right down her legs to meet and overlap the top of her Wellington boots and below the tips of her fingers and almost up to her ears. Only her face and the front of her dark hair were getting really wet.

She stumbled, trying to keep up, and then at last her mother slowed down and shifted her bag, which was full of the pins and measuring tape, the patterns and fabric scraps and chalk, onto the other arm, so she could take hold of Tilly's hand and, as she did so, she squeezed it briefly. It was a squeeze that meant a lot of things, Tilly knew. It meant understanding and friendliness and sharing Tilly's feelings about the walk home in the dark and rain; it meant thank you to Tilly for sitting so long by herself on the tight-buttoned chair in Miss Kendall's parlour and not interrupting at all while Miss Kendall was being measured and fitted and made a fuss of; it meant, everything is all right and we're going home now, it's not too far and we've got one another.

So Tilly squeezed the hand back and her squeeze meant a lot of the same things and a few others of her own besides.

Anyway, she hadn't really minded sitting in Miss Kendall's parlour, though there had been nothing to do there except look at the row of encyclopaedias and piles of old yellow magazines about India and Africa, which were full of pictures that Tilly found either very dull or quite frightening.

They had made up a fire and brought her a glass of milk and a fat square of gingerbread and she had gone off into a peaceful, dreamy state, like a bird hovering on the air, not thinking, not sleeping, just breathing softly. Just *being*.

The parlour was a sad sort of room, as if no one went in there to talk and laugh and leave things lying about. There was a bloom of dust lying over the polish of the table and none of the furniture quite matched, and the pictures on the walls were the sort no one ever wanted to look at but couldn't quite be bothered to get rid of.

Still, she was very used to it, visiting other people's houses with her mother and having to sit quietly in a corner somewhere and not be a nuisance while the customer had a fitting. Very occasionally one of them came to their flat, but Tilly knew her mother didn't encourage that.

'My home is my home,' she said.

But Tilly knew that was not the only reason. There was so little room and most of that was full of the sewing table and the treadle machine, the tailor's dummy and the parcels of cloth and the rail on which the half made-up garments hung.

'People like me to go to their own homes to fit them, in comfort and at their convenience,' Tilly's mother said.

Which was why they were stomping home through all the wind and wet and dark of an evening two weeks before Christmas.

Christmas!

As the word dropped down like a penny into the slot of her mind, Tilly slackened her steps, feeling a spurt of excitement. Perhaps, thanks to Miss Kendall, there might be something special about Christmas this year.

In the spring, she was to be married and Tilly's mother was to make the wedding dress and the bridesmaids' dresses and all the clothes for Miss Kendall's going-away and her honeymoon, which they called her trousseau, and that was a very good order indeed, one of the biggest her mother had ever had. It meant that there would not be worry about the rent and the gas bill and the coal bill and the grocer's bill and Tilly's shoes, for some while. It might even mean there would not be any worry about Christmas.

But Tilly wouldn't mention that, she dared not, only hugged the thought inside her like the coals of a bright small fire that she would keep going herself in private.

THE GLASS ANGELS

There was no one else walking along the esplanade. Only one or two of the street lamps were lit and in between the pools of light they threw on to the pavement there were yards and yards of darkness, like rivers they had to plunge into, Tilly thought, and cross as quickly as possible in order to reach the safety and brightness of the other side.

Along here in summer fairy lights were strung from the trees like the coloured glass beads of a necklace, music and voices came out of the hotels and people strolled up and down, enjoying the warm evening air. But no one came on a seaside holiday in December; the hotels and guest houses were closed and shuttered, though here and there in between them was a tall house in which people lived and a light shone from behind the curtains, making it seem more friendly.

They were walking close to the railings; once or twice Tilly put out her hand to brush against them and a chain of raindrops slid off onto her sleeve. On the other side of the railings, in the darkest of the darkness, lay the gardens and the paths that wound down the cliff to the seashore.

In summer there were miles of flat, honey-coloured sand and the sea lay still and far out and deep blue, there were deck chairs and donkeys, buckets and spades and ice-cream and people, people, people.

How strange it is, Tilly thought, that in the middle of winter the summer seems like a dream, you can hardly imagine it or believe it ever happened, and in summer, you sit on the hot sand in the sunshine and wonder how the winter cold and dark and emptiness could ever, ever have been.

THE GLASS ANGELS

At the end of the esplanade they turned, away from the sound of the sea, which was shut out by tall houses. There were more lights in windows here, a car went by, and a man was walking his dog. It began to feel less lonely. On the corner, the sweet and tobacconist shop was still open, the sweet jars gleaming and glistening like jewels in the window. There were paper chains draped between them. For Christmas.

Past the church and down another road, with front doors set back behind long thin paths which were lined with privet hedges and laurel bushes. Five. Seven. Nine. Home!

They had a privet hedge too, high and straggling, and two stone pillars guarding the gate. It was dark down the path.

Tilly looked up at the window. In that flat Mr and Mrs Day lived, then Miss Brookes, Mrs Plant, Mr Babcock, the people with the one-eyed cat. There was no window for them because their attic flat overlooked the back. But while her mother dug about in her bag for the key and the rain ran down her collar, Tilly was staring up at one particular window. The lamp was on and its shade was a reddish colour, so that its light glowed like the heart of a dark coal in the space where the curtains had been left slightly open. To Tilly, the light was more than a light, it was a message, a warmth, it beckoned her, it promised.

'Come inside Tilly do, no need to get any wetter than you already are, the clothes will take long enough to dry.'

Her mother sounded suddenly weary. Tilly hopped quickly into the hall, the big door shut behind them and they began the trudge up five flights of stairs to the attic. When they reached the second landing, Tilly slowed her steps, wondering, wishing, but her mother frowned and shook her head.

Up another flight. The Babcocks. Then the people with the one-eyed cat.

And then the last steep stairs to their own rooms.

By the time they reached them, of course, the lights had gone out. They always did. You pressed the switch beside the front door and then you had only two minutes to get to the top before it clicked off again by itself.   If she ran fast, two stairs at a time, Tilly could just get to their door before the light went out but her mother climbed much more slowly, especially as she was almost always carrying something, shopping or washing or the sewing bag.

'Why can't there be lights that stay on all the time?'

'Because that would cost Mr Simpkins money and he'd put up the rent to pay for them.'

Mr Simpkins, the hated landlord. All the inconveniences and discomforts of their life seemed to be the fault of Mr Simpkins – leaky taps, draughts, the hole in the floor-board under the sink, the window that rattled, the fact that you had to stand on a wobbly chair to read the gas meter because Mr Simpkins was too mean to get things mended or moved.

And the lights that never stayed on long enough.

But an hour later everything seemed all right again. The coats had been hung up to drip over the bath and the potato pie from yesterday had heated up nicely, with a tin of peas, and then Tilly had not one but two jam tarts because her mother had not wanted hers.

Now, she sat on the rag rug beside the fire, drinking her cocoa and enjoying the pattering of the rain on the roof and the sputtering of the gas and the tok-tok sound of her mother's scissors cutting the cloth that was rolled out across the table – for there was never a time that she was not working. Long after Tilly had gone to bed she would hear the sewing machine, trundle-trundle-trundle, sounding through her dreams.

'Tilly.'

'Oh, not yet, just another few minutes, please.' She had thought that if she stayed still as still she might have been forgotten about altogether and gone to sleep here in the warm instead of having to unwind herself from where she was so comfortable and go off into her icy bedroom.

'Tilly!' Now there was a warning note in her mother's voice.

'All right.'

As she stood up she saw the silk material, shining, creamy-white, and thought of Miss Kendall and her wedding and all the work it meant for her mother. Thought of Christmas. Then she ran into her bedroom and turned on the wash-basin tap quickly before she had time to think about it, carrying a little of the warmth from the sitting room in with her.

THE GLASS ANGELS

When her mother came in to say goodnight, Tilly asked 'Tomorrow after school are we going to do a fitting?'

'No, that was the last for a while. I've just got to get on with the work now. I shall be very busy Tilly.'

'Yes, I know. So please can I go down and see Mrs McBride?'

'You and your Mrs McBride!'

'*Please…*'

Her mother bent over and tucked in Tilly's bedclothes tightly. 'We'll see,' she said but in a voice Tilly knew meant yes.

And then she went out, leaving the door just a little ajar as usual, for Tilly to see a line of light beneath it from across the passage.

CHAPTER TWO

The next school day was a very good one. There was a rehearsal for the Christmas play – Tilly had only a small part, as the innkeeper's wife, but she didn't mind. She loved the whole business of standing up and speaking her line and trying on her costume and watching the others onstage, loved most of all that, even when they were still in school clothes, everyone seemed somehow different and a little strange, part of the other world of the far, hot country and the birth of a baby in a stable, the story-play world, not the ordinary one of here and everyday.

Then, after lunch and a lesson, they had made toffee in the kitchens for the rest of the afternoon and a lot of the toffee turned to fudge but it didn't really matter. They were going to wrap it up in squares of cellophane to be sold next week at the Christmas bazaar, along with the lavender bags and patchwork cushions and fluffy balls made out of bits of wool wound round cardboard circles that they had been making in handicraft all term.

But the pride of Tilly's life was the doll, Victoria Amelia, made and dressed by her own mother, with three changes of clothes, including lacy pantaloons and a tiny fur-trimmed muff. Victoria Amelia was to be raffled. She had been held up at assembly, to the whole school and later put on display in the front hall.

'Oh Christmas, Christmas Christmas,' sang Tilly all the way home.

And she had stopped yet again to admire the sweet jars and chocolate figurines and the paper chains in the window of the corner shop.

'Oh, Christmas, Christmas, Christmas!'

Only the weather didn't feel very Christmassy. It was mild and muggy and the air seemed to be heavy and fill your lungs like bathroom steam and there was a constant drizzle.

Christmas ought to be snow – snow and ice over the puddles and frost fingered into feathers on the window panes and sharp, bright cold. That was how it was in books, that was how they sang it every day in the play practices.

'Deep and crisp and even…'

'Frosty winds made moan…'

That was how it ought to be.

'Be careful!' her mother shouted out as Tilly ran up the last flight of stairs.

'Be careful as you come in.'

When she opened the door she saw why.

'Oh, it's beautiful!'

The silk for Miss Kendall's wedding dress was unrolled over the table, and cascading down in soft shining folds to the floor. The chairs had been pushed back and an old clean sheet spread over the carpet.

'You'll have to have your tea in the kitchen, Tilly, I can't risk anything being spilled in here. I'll clear it away soon but I do just want to finish marking it out.'

'I don't mind.'

She didn't. She liked to stand in the tiny kitchen that was partitioned off from the living room and so narrow there was no space for a table or chair, just a cupboard with a worktop beside the sink. But between the two was a space into which she could still just manage to squeeze, and then she could stand at the long window and look out, down into the yard below or else over the rooftops and up at the sky. Even when it was dark she liked it, liked the moonlight and the stars and the oblongs of light that shone out from the windows below.

But tonight the drizzle and mist made them fuzzy and bleared the windowpane.

Tilly took her plate of bread and jam and a slab of marble cake and ate quickly, and gulped down her milk, partly because she was hungry and school dinner hours ago, but much more, because she wanted to be off, down the stairs and knocking on the magic door.

'Can I go and see Mrs McBride?'

'If you bolt your food like that you'll get indigestion.'

'No, I won't I never do.'

'Now Miss Clever…'

'Can I *go*?'

Her mother looked at her. Her hand was resting on the beautiful silk.

'I'd be out of your way, wouldn't I?' Tilly said, 'You could get the pattern marked out.'

'Yes.' A shadow crossed her mother's face, though whether it was of worry or sadness Tilly couldn't tell.

'Poor Tilly,' she said, it's a bit miserable for you I know, always having to make room for the sewing. If we just had a bit more space…' She didn't bother to finish because they both knew there was no point. Larger flats cost more rent and they didn't have the money.

'If I could get a few more orders like this one for Miss Kendal – the trouble is, I've only got one pair of hands.'

She held one of them out and Tilly went to her, stepping very carefully round the silk, and her mother hugged her for a minute.

'But I don't want to neglect you.'

'You don't. I'm all right.'

'Are you? Did you have a good day at school?'

'Lovely,' And she told her mother quickly about the play rehearsal and the toffee-making.'

And everybody thinks Victoria Amelia is beautiful, they all want to win her.'

'Well, if she makes a pound or two more.'

The Christmas bazaar was to raise money for refugees who had been forced to flee their own countries during the war and still had no proper homes. They should do whatever they could, Tilly's mother had said.

'It might have been us, Tilly. We could easily have been refugees, if men like your father hadn't died fighting for their country.'

'Yes, I know.' Tilly said and pulled quickly away. She didn't like it when her mother talked like that, it gave her a strange feeling in her tummy. Her father had been killed when she was a tiny baby. She had never seen him.

She felt confused too because a part of her knew she should be proud of her father for dying and helping the war to be won – she had been told so enough times – but another part of her was angry with him for leaving them, so that her mother had to work and work and they still had so little money and had to live in a tiny attic flat with horrible Mr Simpkins for a landlord. Surely it had been a bit of

his own fault? Lots of other soldiers and sailors and airmen had come home so why couldn't he have been more careful not to get killed?

But those were thoughts she could never, ever speak.

'Please can I go to see Mrs McBride now? *Pleeeese…*'

'Go on then but not for too long and if it isn't convenient for her.'

'I'm to come straight back, I know, I know.'

And so Tilly escaped to run down the two flights

of stairs and along the short passage to the door of Mrs McBride's flat. It was always kept on the latch and Tilly had agreed on a special way of knocking so that Mrs McBride would know it was her.

Rat-ta-ta-TAT – the first three taps light the last much heavier. It was the V for Victory signal, Mrs McBride had told her, they had played it every night on the wireless during the dark days of the war.

Rat-ta-ta-TAT.

'Come in.'

Whenever she opened Mrs McBride's door Tilly always paused and stood on the inner door mat and closed her eyes, to sniff in the special and particular

　　　　　THE GLASS ANGELS

smell of this flat. Most places had their own smell – their flat smelled of material and sewing-machine oil, the school hall smelled of polish and wood, her grandmother's house in Tenfield had smelled of coal smoke and soot.

But Mrs McBride's smelled of – what exactly? Ginger biscuits, Tilly had finally decided. Ginger biscuits and violet-scented soap, mixed with a trace of candle wax, a trace of silver polish and a trace of horsehair. Altogether it was so powerful and pleasing that Tilly like to fill her nose with it the second she arrived. I'm here, she thought. I'm really here.

Then she crossed the hall and pushed hard against the sitting room door so that the draught-excluder sausage dog moved out of the way.

Mrs McBride was lame. She could get up and walk stiffly across the room using her two sticks, but most of the time she stayed in her chair, which was either turned to face the window or the fire, with her feet up on a little round beaded stool.

The room was actually quite large – much larger than their own in the attic, but Mrs McBride had so many things crowded into it, and particularly some very big, dark pieces of furniture, that it seemed small and cramped. Every corner had something in it, everywhere you looked there were treasures. Tilly thought she could come and sit here every day for a year and still not see everything.

In the centre of the room was the great round polished table on which stood a blue and white patterned bowl and which had six chairs round it. Apart from Mrs McBride's armchair, there were two others, and a deep soft sofa covered in cushions, round and square, large and small, cushions embroidered, tapestried, flowered, silk, satin, velvet and wool. There were other footstools too, one embroidered with an elephant carrying a howdah on its back, and a brown leather pouffe. A tall, glass-fronted cabinet against one wall was filled with china ornaments and figurines, with flower-patterned plates, cups, bowls, dishes and jugs, and another against the opposite wall which displayed glass, deep blue and ruby red and clear crystal. There were small tables draped with cloths that fell to the floor, on which stood pictures in silver frames, photographs of babies in christening robes and brides in huge, flower-brimmed hats, and soldiers with medals and moustaches. They were all of them from Mrs McBride's family, with animals, too, several small dogs and a white pony harnessed to a cart.

Beside Mrs McBride's chair next to the fire were low cupboards and inside them, more treasures, boxes filled with beads and buttons, pictures sewn in silk, fans, old post cards, a miniature set of farmyard animals, scraps of material from old wedding dresses and christening robes, and even a piece of ribbon that had come from an evening gown worn by Queen Victoria.

Every time Tilly went, Mrs McBride would bring out a different box and with each box came a story.

Once, she said, she had lived in a very large house with a long drive, and a morning room, a drawing room, her own private sitting room, a breakfast room and a parlour. There had been maids and a butler, a cook and two gardeners and a nursemaid, and up to ten guests to stay every Friday to Monday.

But then Mrs McBride's husband had died and her children had grown.

'And times changed and I rattled round in that house like a marble in a bread-crock,' she had told Tilly. So she had moved to a smaller house.

'But one of Hitler's bombs flattened that, so here I am. Which is plenty of space for one old woman to take up in an overcrowded world.'

Now, Mrs McBride turned as Tilly came in.

'Ah, there you are. If you would please put a wee speck of coal on that fire it would look more cheerful.'

So Tilly did, and scraped away some of the cinders and ash beneath with the edge of the poker so that the flames came spurting through and the coal began to crackle.

'Well, that is much better and brighter on a dark wet night. Thank you Matilda. And how are you?'

She was the only person in the world who ever called Tilly by her full and proper name and the only one, Tilly's mother said, who would be allowed by Tilly to get away with it, for she had been Tilly from the day she was born to everyone; not many people even knew she was really called anything different.

'But Matilda is your christened name and a good one and I had a sister called Matilda,' Mrs McBride said one day when Tilly had first begun to come down to her flat.

'Where is she now?'

'She died of scarlet fever at the age of two, which was a terrible thing and a great sadness.'

'Children did die of things then. More than nowadays,' Tilly had said.

'But never let anyone tell you that it didn't matter so much, because it did. Women bore eight and lost four but every one of them was loved and grieved over, every one was precious.'

'Like Matilda.'

'Like her.'

Now, Tilly settled on the floor and began to fiddle with the fringing on a rug that was spread over the armchair as she told about the nativity play and the carol service and the Christmas bazaar and after all that about the wedding dress for Miss Kendall, and as Mrs McBride listened her plump fingers went stiffly in and out of her crochet and her rings glinted in the firelight and the oil painting of the Cavalier in the lace collar looked down at them benignly from its place above the mantle.

Later, Mrs McBride sent Tilly to the kitchen for the tin where the marshmallows were kept and they toasted them on a brass fork over the fire.

They dissolved sweetly, softly, stickily in their mouths and Mrs McBride drank her very small glass of Madeira wine to go with them. Tilly felt herself wrapped in quietness and comfort, warmth and contentment.

They talked of a great many things, but most of all they talked about Christmas.

'In the window of the sweetie shop there are baubles made out of chocolate, wrapped in shiny paper and marzipan snowmen, and they've hung paper chains round the jars and the grocer has boxes of Christmas crackers.

'Ah,' said Mrs McBride, 'but you should have seen

the windows of the big department stores before the war."

Her fingers worked in and out of the crochet and the firelight gleamed on the gold frames of her spectacles.

'Tell me,' Tilly said, and tucked her legs up more tightly beneath her. She liked to hear Mrs McBride's stories about being a child in the country, and about the grand parties she had held in her married house, but most of all, she liked to hear about 'before the war' which she always thought of as one long word. Her own mother talked about it sometimes too. Beforethewar was a magical time, before the long dark days and nights of bombs and blitz and blackout, of gas masks and air-rid sirens and queues and rationing and fathers gone for soldiers.

'At Christmas beforethewar,' said Mrs McBride, 'when there was plenty of everything, the windows of all the big stores had tableaux – scenes from storybooks, fairy tales and pantomime and nursery rhymes, with models of woodcutters and pixies and gingerbread houses and Santa Claus's workshop and elfin glades and Puss in Boots and Aladdin's cave and the Snow Queen and – oh, anything you could

dream of. And the models moved – wheels turned and axes chopped and snowflakes fell and stars twinkled and everything was lit from within, they all shone out into the darkness of the street; and then inside the shops the goods were piled high, the crystallised fruits and jars of ginger, brandied cherries and sugared almonds and cakes with icing and scarlet ribbons. Oh and the toys! Such toys as *you* never saw, Tilly – dolls dressed in satin ball-gowns and Ascot hats, baby dolls and sailors dolls, and then

THE GLASS ANGELS

dolls' houses with real, working lights, and dolls' prams. Teddy bears as big as ponies and lions made out of real fur and clockwork trains and forts full of soldiers, farmyards full of animals, model yachts to sail on the pond. I remember all the fruit too – not just apples and pears, but pineapples and figs and bananas from overseas, all heaped up, and sacks of nuts and wooden boxes of dates and muscatels.'

'Oh, I wish it was still Beforethewar,' Tilly said, looking into the fire and trying to imagine the shop windows with their tableaux, the lights and the gold and silver decorations.

'Well, I daresay it will all come back one of these days and more besides. But just now, Matilda, if you open the cupboard and take out my box that is tied with green string … I went looking in the bottom of the trunk this morning.'

Mrs McBride often 'went looking in the bottom of the trunk,' though it seemed to Tilly that the trunk could not actually have a bottom and must be the size of a cellar too, so many things came out of it, and there were always plenty more.

Now, she found the box and gave it to Mrs McBride and then sat back on her heels while the green string was carefully unpicked and rolled up into a ball and the box lid taken off.

Inside she could see little mounds of yellowy-white tissue paper. Out came the first, then another and another and Mrs McBride began carefully to unwrap each one. It took some time and Tilly's eyes never left the box and as she saw what was there she felt all the usual surprise and delight that came whenever Mrs McBride found something in her cupboard, or in a drawer, or opened a box or an envelope, for every time it contained something beautiful or astonishing, funny or strange and always like nothing Tilly had ever seen in her life before.

There had been a fan made of ostrich feathers and a watch-case of gold, shawls embroidered all over with black beads and a tumbling monkey, a jewel box of satin set inside a bird's egg, a wooden doll the size of her fingernail holding a baby doll the size of an orange pip.

'Go and switch off the big light, Matilda, if you please.'

Tilly went to the other side of the room and reached up. 'There now,' Mrs McBride said.

And Tilly turned and looked round.

On the small table beside Mrs McBride's chair, in the pool of light from the lamp, stood a slender column, with arms stretching out all round it like the graceful branches of a tree. The whole thing was made of sparkling clear crystal glass. But it might have been made of ice, Tilly thought, because it glistened too in just that way. Suspended from each of the branches by a silver thread as fine as a spider's were angels, and the angels were made of crystal too, with outstretched wings and haloes and robes that were swept up into an arc at the side. The crystal was cut into patterns all over, like the goblets in Mrs McBride's cabinet.

The whole thing was turning very slowly and as it turned, the wings and haloes and outstretched robes of the angels caught the light and sparkled and glittered and the column gleamed and shone and music came tinkling from the revolving base, the music of the Rocking Carol.

Tilly crept softly across the room and stood close beside the table, holding her breath for fear that the whole thing might break in pieces or vanish.

'Oh, beautiful!' she whispered. 'Oh, beautiful!' and together, she and Mrs McBride watched as the shining crystal angels turned and turned, and looking at Mrs McBride's face, Tilly saw that she was far away from this room and this time, was somewhere else, with other people, remembering, remembering.

CHAPTER THREE

That night, Tilly lay in bed listening to the rain on the roof and, when she closed her eyes, seeing the crystal angels turning and sparkling. Her mother was still sewing, pinning up the wedding dress on the tailor's dummy. She would get undressed in the dark and slip into the other bed long after Tilly had gone to sleep.

But tonight she had said that there was just one more day of work on it and then she would stop and get ready for Christmas. She would come to the play and the bazaar and the carol service, and then it would be the last day of term, when Tilly would break up from school at lunchtime.

'And in the afternoon we'll go Christmas shopping!'

'Can we have a tree this year, a real one with ornaments – just a small one, in the corner?'

But the answer had been the usual one. 'We'll see.'

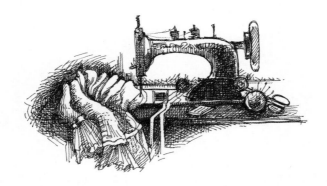

There was already a cake though, that had been made in October and stored away in a tin to mature. In a few days' time, they would ice it.

They had spent last Christmas at Tadfield with her mother's cousin, Eleanor Flint. She had made Tilly call her 'Aunt Flint.' It had not been a very happy time. Tilly's mother and Aunt Flint did not get on and the house had been cold and polished and very tidy. There had been no decorations other than a single line of Christmas cards on the mantelpiece.

The dressmaking business had been very slack all that year. There had been a lot of the hated renovations and alterations which were more trouble than they were worth and paid very little. Tilly's presents had been a pair of woollen gloves and a pencil case, plus a red book of stories which had belonged to Aunt Flint when she was a girl. Aunt

Flint had questioned her the whole time about what she did at school and complained that she was too precocious and banged doors.

'Next year, we'll stay at home, just the two of us,' Tilly's mother had said tightening her lips. But even that did not sound very exciting.

Mrs McBride was going to spend three days with friends; she was to be fetched by car. Tilly tried not to think about it. She did not want the lamp not to be shining through the chink in the curtains and the flat to be empty and closed-up when she passed.

'We must take down a Christmas dinner for Miss Brooks,' her mother had said. 'She has no one at all in the world, poor soul. I'd ask her up here but she would never manage the stairs.'

Tilly prayed that she wouldn't have to take the dinner down, as she sometimes had to take odd bits of shopping. She was afraid of Miss Brooks. Her flat had a bead curtain over the kitchen doorway, that clacked softly, and it smelled sour. Miss Brooks talked to herself, had dirty fingernails and wild eyes and gypsy earrings, and a shrieking parrot in a cage that was hardly ever cleaned out. Tilly's mother said that Miss Brooks was just very lonely and neglected and rather forgetful, but Tilly always tried to get away as quickly as she could in case Miss Brooks should catch her and hold her by the arm with fingers that gripped as tight as claws.

To stop herself thinking about it, she turned over in bed and made the picture of the glass angels come before her eyes and then tried to remember all the things Mrs McBride had said used to be in the shops Beforethewar. She wanted to dream about those, not about Miss Brooks and the terrible parrot.

The school nativity play was a great success and at the bazaar a girl in Tilly's class called Bettina Truman won the doll Victoria Amelia. She was so overcome with surprise and pleasure that she grabbed Tilly round the waist and danced her all the way down the school hall. When they got back up to the top again, out of breath, she said, 'And I want you to come to my Boxing Day party. I've told my mother and you have to ask yours. It's going to be really good, with an entertainer and an ice-cream cake but you will have to wear pumps and a best frock. Have you got a best frock?'

Tilly stood up very straight. 'Of course I have.'

'That's all right then.'

But Tilly saw the familiar look of anxiety cross her mother's face when she told her.

'Your best frock is two years' old, it's much too small for you now and I haven't time to make you another, and you don't have any pumps – would slippers do? And they live at Uplands don't they, one of those big houses on the cliff beyond Miss Kendall's? There wouldn't be any buses on Boxing Day so we would have to walk and…' Her voice trailed off. But then she smiled at Tilly.

'But there, I expect we can manage somehow if you really do want to go. I didn't know Bettina Truman was a special friend of yours.'

'Yes, she is,' said Tilly quickly.

It was a lie though. She hardly knew Bettina Truman, who had only been at the school for two years, and did not really like her. She had felt a thud of disappointment in her stomach when Bettina's name had been read out as the winner of the doll Victoria Amelia.

The worst had been when Bettina had called Tilly a 'free place child' and lots of the class had turned round to stare.

'What is a 'free place child'?' Tilly had demanded, bursting into the flat that afternoon, 'and am I one?'

Her mother had lain down her dressmaking scissors, looking upset. 'Yes,' she had said quietly, 'Yes, Tilly, you are. There are a few free places at your school for girls who deserve to have a good education but whose families can't afford the fees.'

'Because their fathers were killed in the war like mine?'

'Yes, or sometimes for other reasons. It isn't anything to be ashamed of Tilly, but I would like to know how it got out and who it was told you.'

But Tilly had refused to say.

Now though, the thought of the Boxing Day party made her push it all the way down to the bottom of her mind. The party shone out like a beacon. She would wear a best frock, she knew her mother would manage something, and perhaps even buy her some pumps out of Miss Kendall's money, for surely she must understand that to go in furry slippers would be truly awful.

On the day of the Carol service, Tilly's mother had

a cough at breakfast that even three cups of tea did not soothe. She sat at the back of the church, which was very cold indeed, and Tilly could see her coughing into her handkerchief so as not to make a disturbance. On the way home her face was flushed and her eyes oddly bright.

'I'm afraid I'm going down with a bad cold Tilly.'

'But you'll be better tomorrow won't you?'

'Oh yes, I expect so, but I think it would be a good idea if I went to bed early tonight with a hot drink and an aspirin. Will you be all right?'

'Of course I will.'

Tilly felt important as she helped her mother to bed, as if she were grown-up and in charge of things now, though inside herself she felt a bit uncertain. She could not remember her mother being ill like this ever before.

All that night she coughed and the next morning she was obviously worse. When she got out of bed to go to the bathroom she had to clutch hold of the bed because she felt giddy.

'I don't think I can stand up, Tilly — I think this must be influenza not just a cold. I do feel quite poorly.'

'What shall I do?' Tilly asked anxiously, 'Should I go and tell Mrs McBride? Shall I go out to the telephone box and ring the doctor?'

'Oh no, no, I'll be fine, I'll just go back to sleep. I'm sure that will get me better. But you'll have to make your own breakfast and get yourself ready for school. Can you manage? And we won't be able to go shopping this afternoon as I promised.'

'Will you better tomorrow?'

'Oh yes, of course I will.'

But Tilly didn't think that she sounded very certain.

The last morning of term and all the excitement of breaking up for the Christmas holidays lost some of its edge because Tilly was worrying about her mother and wondering what would happen, what she should do… There wasn't much time left to get ready and what if…She knew she ought only to think of her mother being ill, only she felt that she could not bear it if, when this Christmas had promised to be so special, suddenly there was to be no Christmas for them at all.

She ran all the way home from the bus through

the early dark and drizzle, not even stopping to look in the corner sweetie shop.

Her mother seemed very ill indeed.

'Tilly, I think perhaps you had better ring the doctor. There's some change for the telephone in my purse. And would you go to the grocer's, we need bread and cheese and some eggs and perhaps get a bottle of lemon barley, I'm so thirsty.'

All the time she was talking she coughed and her face looked shiny and damp and her eyes seemed to have gone darker and sunken down into her head.

Tilly made herself a jam sandwich with the last of the loaf and went out, eating it from her hand.

She didn't care about Christmas now because she was so frightened. Her mother looked so ill and her father was dead already, so what if…

She stood stock still in the roadway.

If her mother died, she would have no one at all except Aunt Flint, in the cold house in Tadfield.

She began to run, clutching the coins tightly in her hand. By the time she reached the telephone kiosk she had to get her breath before she could speak to the person who answered at Dr Craddock's.

*

'Hm,' he said, as he sat by her mother's bed later, his hand on the pulse at her wrist. She was lying still now but when Tilly had got back she had been tossing about, throwing back the bedcovers and muttering to herself. Once she had cried out and Tilly had gone in to her but it was as though her mother could not see her, she had stared through her somehow before falling back against the pillows.

'Tilly, your mother is really quite ill. I don't like the sound of her chest at all and she has a very high fever – she could be in for pneumonia.'

Dr Craddock looked at Tilly intently. Tilly had known him ever since she could remember – he had sorted out her mumps and measles and croup and tonsillitis and put stitches in her lip when she had fallen. Now she saw how serious his face was and a cold feeling ran down her spine. Then he stood up and beckoned her into the sitting room.

'We'll leave her to sleep.'

He sat down on the arm of a chair.

'She is going to die isn't she?' The inside of Tilly's mouth felt dry as she spoke.

'No, no, she won't die but she is very ill and I'm concerned about you here alone. Is there no one who could come and stay?'

'No, we don't have anybody.'

Tilly pushed the thought of Aunt Flint away. 'I can look after her if you tell me what to do.'

'I was really thinking she should be sent to hospital.'

'Oh please, not, she'd hate that and she *can't* be in hospital for Christmas. Besides, if she did…'

'Then what would happen to you?'

'I can give her medicine and get her drinks, I can help her to wash. I can light the gas and make eggs on toast and come to the telephone if she gets worse. And there are people in the other flats.'

'Well… that is true I suppose…' He hesitated a moment, then stood up.

'And I will come in every day Tilly. I'll leave two bottles of medicine now. Try to see she has plenty to drink but otherwise let her sleep, and if you're worried about anything at all, ring my home. Have you enough coins for the telephone?'

When Dr Craddock had gone Tilly went into the kitchen and stood in the window space looking out. It was dark now and still raining. The sound of it running down the gutters was comforting and made her feel less alone. But after a time she felt afraid about things again. Her mother was sleeping. Tilly put a jug of barley water and a glass beside her bed and a note in case she woke, and slipped downstairs, leaving the door on the latch.

'I mustn't stay for long,' she said, standing on the hearthrug beside Mrs McBride's chair.

And then she poured out everything, about her mother's illness that the doctor feared might turn to pneumonia and what else he had said, and old Mrs McBride's hands lay still on her crochet as she listened.

'And she won't be able to go out and in three days it will be Christmas – only it won't, we shant have a Christmas shall we, not at all? Oh it isn't fair, it isn't fair!'

Tilly cried then, not only tears of worry and fear but of anger too.

Mrs McBride waited until she had quietened down.

'Well now, Matilda, you'll feel much better after that. Poor you – and your poor mother. Not much of a Christmas for her either.'

'No,' Tilly said, blowing her nose.

'Now, go into my kitchen and look in the cupboard on the wall, to the right. You will see a bottle of linctus.'

When Tilly brought it, Mrs McBride said, 'That mixture has cured a good many coughs and nasty chests – it will do your mother a power of good. Now, under a cloth in the larder is half an apple pie. I ate mine for lunch and your mother will not be feeling like any but I daresay you will. Put a drop of top-of-the-milk on it. The third thing is over there on the sideboard. I've been to the bottom of the old trunk again.'

It was another of the brown cardboard boxes tied with green string.

'Now those,' Mrs McBride said, ' we had on the Christmas tree at my married home every single year and a couple of them when I was a child long before that. The others were lost when the bomb fell so these are the last few.'

Carefully, one by one, Tilly took out seven Christmas tree ornaments. They felt so light and so fragile in her hand she was afraid they might break just by being touched. There were two gold and two silver spheres on fine thread, a tiny holly tree with red berries, fashioned out of glass, a bird with a long tail feather of peacock green and an iridescent sheen over its body, and a glass star with fine silver brushwork on the points.

'You may not be having a tree,' Mrs McBride said, 'but you could surely find some place to hang them – or just set them on the windowsill to catch the light.'

'Thank you.' Tilly said. 'Oh, they're lovely and I will be very careful with them.'

Upstairs she ate the apple pie with some cheese and a piece of chocolate she found at the back of the drawer. Her mother had a drink and a spoonful of Mrs McBride's linctus as well as more of the doctor's medicine. The linctus looked horrible, dark treacly brown and sticky and her mother said it was bitter

THE GLASS ANGELS

and puckered her mouth up when she swallowed it, but before long she slept again more peacefully, though she still looked very pale, and thinner, Tilly thought, thinner and older.

'Tilly, are you all right my love? What is happening abut everything?'

But she did not wait for an answer or seem to have the strength to go on worrying, just turned her head on the pillow again and closed her eyes.

Tilly lit the gas fire, then sat beside it with her book in her lap. But she couldn't take in what she was reading properly, and in the end she gave up and just sat, wondering. Tomorrow, she thought, she could go out to the shops herself to buy whatever they needed, the Christmas chicken and vegetables, and if her mother told her how, surely she would be able to cook them. She could buy fruit and perhaps some sweets and there was the Christmas cake ready to be eaten. Dr Craddock would come again and ten surely her mother would be better? It would all be fine so long as she did not have to go into hospital and Tilly be sent to Aunt Flint.

But oh, it did not seem like Christmas, she

thought, and wished that there might be snow and then at least it would look right. She went to the window again. 'At least it would feel like Christmas,' she said aloud.

But there was only the rain, more and more of it, and the darkness and the wind, so that in the end, Tilly drew the curtains tightly and went to bed, feeling lonelier than she had ever done in her life.

As she crossed the room she passed close to Miss Kendall's wedding dress, cut out, tacked and pinned up on the dummy with the cascade of silk lace that would form the train spreading out behind. Tilly touched it lightly. It felt cold and yet warm too, slippery-smooth yet with a slight roughness that caught against the pads of her fingers.

When it was finished it would have embroidery and beading and a scalloped hem, with fine seaming at the neck and cuffs and on the bodice and Miss Kendall would look like a bride in a fairy story.

Now, on the stand, the half-made dress gleamed pale and ghost-like, and all at once Tilly wished it were not there like some silent, dead thing, and she went quickly into the bedroom and closed the door.

CHAPTER FOUR

She woke with a start and sat up. Her mother was coughing again but when Tilly spoke to her softly she did not reply. It must have been the rain that had woken her, that and the wind beating at the windows. But it seemed to her that she had heard another sound too, a creak or a crack. Now though, there was nothing and after a while she lay down again and burrowed deep under the bedclothes not only for warmth but for comfort. She had a feeling of loneliness, like hunger gnawing inside her.

When she slept again dreams came crowding in on her, confused, peculiar and frightening. It was as though she knew she was asleep and was trying to bring herself awake but could not.

The next morning was dark but at last the rain had stopped. She would get up and make her mother a cup of tea. Perhaps she would be better today – though in her heart Tilly knew that even if she were better would still not mean she would be well enough for them to have a proper Christmas.

Only it did not seem to matter so much now. Her mother's illness had frightened Tilly. All she wanted now was for it to be over and her mother to be well.

She got out of bed, went across the passage and opened the sitting room door. And then she gave a cry – except that the cry did not come out properly but seemed to stick in her throat and did not come out. She simply stood in horror, staring and staring.

There had been a long crack across the ceiling of the living room ever since Tilly could remember – she had always thought of it as a friendly sort of crack. But now it was not friendly at all, it was much wider, ugly and jagged and some of the plaster around it had broken away and fallen. Dirty water was dripping steadily through the crack – it looked as if it had been dripping through all night, onto the tailor's dummy and Miss Kendall's white silk wedding dress and the train and the roll of material spread out on the floor behind it. The dress was quite wet and stained with dark brown, muddy stains.

There was a puddle on the train and the carpet all around was wet too and lumps of plaster and dirt lay on it and on the table.

Tilly knew, even in the midst of her shock and confusion, that she ought to put something under the hole to catch any more rain that might begin to fall again and she went to the kitchen and got a bowl, and the tin bucket from under the sink. But she had no idea how to begin to clear up the mess. Whatever happened, her mother must not find out, not yet, while she was still so ill – Tilly knew she must keep it from her. It was not the ceiling that mattered or even the carpet and the chair, it was that Miss

Kendall's wedding dress was completely ruined – and Tilly had heard her mother say that the silk alone had cost forty pounds. And where would another forty pounds come from?

Then she realised as she stood in the middle of the sitting room among the plaster and water and ruined dress that she did not know what more she could do. She could not manage alone any more. Her mother being ill, and Christmas in two days' time had been bad enough but this was quite different.

Perhaps it was her fault that the plaster had fallen in, perhaps she should have noticed that something was wrong last night.

She felt muddled and frightened, but beneath all of that which was churning up her tummy like a stormy sea, she felt strangely calm and sure, suddenly, about what she must do first, and for the best. She went quietly into the bedroom and got dressed and then stuffed her pillow down inside her bed and pulled the covers right up. In the grey light of early morning it might look to her mother as if she was still in bed, humped up asleep.

'Please don't let her find it,' she said, in an urgent, whispered-aloud prayer. 'Please let her stay asleep.'

And then she went, pulling on her Mac and boots in the hallway and running down all the flights of stairs in the dark in case the click of the light switch should wake her mother. At the end of the corridor that led to Mrs McBride's she hesitated. But Mrs McBride could not climb up the stairs with her or go out for help, she was an old lady, she was for visiting and talking to and telling things and being with companionably, but this was different.

The streets were quiet, the curtains still drawn at windows. No one was about. It had not begun to rain again, but as the dawn seeped up over the sea, Tilly saw that the sky was full of great-bellied, scudding clouds and when she turned onto the Esplanade, the sea was white flecked and heaving about within itself.

It seemed further than she had remembered and she wished she had a bicycle and though she ran for quite a way, she eventually got a stitch in her side so that she had to slow down to a walk again.

A short way up the last stretch of the hill towards Cliff House, a small brown dog appeared out of some bushes and ran alongside her and Tilly felt cheered by it and hoped it would keep her company all the way, but when she reached the top of the sea-front road and turned left, it scampered away, answering a distant whistle.

She had never been as far as this by herself. Perhaps, if circumstances had been different, she might have enjoyed it, smelling the salt on the air and feeling independent, passing the closed-up hotels and dreaming of summer. But now she was hardly aware of her surroundings, she was simply kept going by the urgency of where she had to go and why.

Then she reached the big, double-fronted house and saw a light on and felt her heart pounding as she scrunched and scrambled her way up the gravel drive to the steps and the front door. She pulled the brass bell knob hard and heard it jangling far inside. A man opened the door, a small, bald man with a moustache. He was wearing a red dressing-gown.

'Well bless me,' he said, looking Tilly closely up and down, 'Who in heaven's name are you?'

'I'm Tilly,' she said, 'and I...'

She faltered and began again.

'My name is Matilda Cumberland and please may I see Miss Kendall – it's... It's very important.'

And then, without any warning to herself at all, she had burst into tears.

Behind the man, as he shepherded her into the house, she heard a voice and then saw a woman, though not Miss Kendall.

'Good gracious Gerald, I think it's the dressmaker's child!'

When they had been to this house before, for Miss Kendall to choose patterns and be measured, Miss Kendall's mother had been quite kind to Tilly, but distant – her smile had not been the sort of smile that meant warmth and friendship, just politeness. Tilly thought they were rich and grand and snobbish and she had not liked the way Mrs Kendall had called her 'the dressmaker's child' just then.

But whatever they thought of her, they showed only concern and helpfulness now. Tilly was taken not into the little back parlour but the dining room where there was a fire and silver candlesticks and a Christmas tree in the window and breakfast was set out and they made her have hot milk with honey stirred into it and porridge with cream, and Miss Kendall was fetched down and sat beside her and her hair floated loose onto her shoulders and she looked younger and somehow softer, Tilly thought. Her brother was there too, Mr Alec Kendall, and he waved a slice of toast at Tilly and winked and spoke with his mouth full.

But it was hard to smile or swallow the food she was so afraid, full of the enormity of what had happened and the awfulness of what she had to tell

them. Yet when at last she did, pouring it all out in a
great rush, somehow it was all right in spite of the
way they sat round her and stared at her in silence as
she spoke.

'And your mother hadn't woken up when you
came out, so she doesn't know about any of this?'
asked Mr Kendall.

'No, but she might have woken up now, I have to
go back.' She turned to Miss Kendall. 'You see, the
dress is completely spoiled, that's what I had to come
and tell you, its wet and covered with dirt and plaster,
I shouldn't think any of the material could be saved
and Mother said it cost forty pounds. Only she
doesn't have forty pounds, she couldn't buy any

more herself and the money she was earning for making the dress was going to pay the bills and some of it was for a proper Christmas too.'

She swallowed hard and dug her fingers into the palms of her hands but it was no use at all, she couldn't stop herself from crying all over again.

After that a great many things happened, a tumble of things one after another and in the end Tilly just gave up and let them, because the Kendalls seemed to know best and to want to take charge and sort everything out.

Telephone calls were made and Miss Kendall went away to get dressed and her brother persuaded Tilly to eat a peach and the juice ran down her chin and he threw her his napkin to mop it up and winked at her again. She had only tasted a real peach, not one out of a tin, once in her life before and that had been in the summer, so that ever afterwards, Tilly was to think of rich people as the ones who had peaches to eat in December.

After a while the Kendalls' car was brought round and on the way home they called in at a builder's yard where Mr Kendall had a talk with the builder about the cracks in the ceiling where the water had come

THE GLASS ANGELS

in, and in another few minutes they were swishing through the puddles up to the block of flats.

'I'll go first,' Tilly said, scrambling out. She had liked the car. It had smelled of leather and oil and the seats were squashy and cool against the backs of her legs, but there had been a rug to put over her knees to keep the fronts of them warm as toast.

'I'll go first in case...' and Miss Kendall nodded and touched her shoulder reassuringly.

As soon as they neared the last flight of stairs Tilly heard her mother coughing, coughing and crying.

She was sitting on the chair beside the table in her night-dress, amongst the rubble and plaster and the rain dripping into the bowl and bucket, and the spoiled wedding-dress. For a moment, seeing Tilly, she looked frightened and her face was as pale as the ghostly silk, but then she reached out for Tilly's hand and held onto it and she could do nothing else but cry while Tilly knelt down beside her stroking her arm. 'It's all right, she said, 'it's all going to be all right now,' and she had a strange sensation of having changed places with her mother, done all her growing-up overnight so that she was the one who knew what to do and was in charge and her mother was a helpless child.

The rest of the day was a confusion of comings and goings. The flat had never been so full of so many people. The doctor came and the builder, who was called Mr Rourke, and then Mr Simpkins their landlord, and he seemed a very different man from the way he usually was with Tilly's mother, one who talked respectfully to Mr and Miss Kendall. A grocer's delivery van and a butcher's boy arrived with parcels and boxes of food, and later a nurse that the doctor and Miss Kendall had arranged for appeared. She gave Tilly's mother a wash and changed her bed sheets, took her temperature and settled her down again on plumped-up pillows. She was a little better, Dr Craddock said. While she had slept her body had fought a battle against the infection and begun to win. But she was still quite ill and must be properly looked after by the nurse.

'In hospital?" Tilly asked anxiously.

'Well, she doesn't really need that now, but…'

'She certainly doesn't,' Miss Kendall said, 'she must come to us at Cliff House. There are plenty of spare rooms and the nurse can come every day. She and Tilly can spend Christmas with us.'

For a moment it seemed to Tilly that there was nothing she could do, it had all been taken out of their hands and settled and perhaps it would be a good thing and her mother would have a chance to get properly well and the Kendalls had such a beautiful house and a Christmas tree and peaches...

She sat down. Mr Kendall had gone downstairs with Mr Simpkins and the builder was starting to clear all the plaster rubble into a sack. He whistled 'Good King Wenceslas and The Holly and the Ivy as he did it. Tilly liked him.

'What's going to happen to the ceiling?' she asked.

'Oh we'll patch it up to keep the old rain out for now. Next week I'll be back to fix it good and proper.' He made it sound as if it were nothing to him, just nothing at all, when Tilly had wondered that morning whether the whole house would collapse, so that they would have to find somewhere else to live.

'Made a proper old mess,' Mr Rourke said 'but things generally look worse than they are you see.'

The ceiling was looking better already. The hole

didn't seem nearly so gaping or the cracks so wide or the pile of rubble so huge,

'Will it cost a lot to mend?'

He winked. 'Cost your old landlord a bob or two but that's his worry, isn't it?'

So Mr Kendall really had dealt with Mr Simpkins. Everything seemed to be running away like an express train and Tilly knew she ought to be grateful and she was, she was. Only...

'Tilly? Tilly, where are you?'

Her mother was propped up on two pillows. Her hair was brushed neatly back from her forehead and her face had just a very little colour in it again. The nurse had set out her medicines and a jug of fresh barley water covered with a cloth, and a sponge in a bowl, neatly on the bedside able. She would be back that evening, she had said. Tilly sat on the edge of the bed.

'Do you feel better?'

'Yes I do. I feel weak but having the nurse and knowing everything is being sorted out and that you're all right Tilly...'

'Yes.'

'They have all been very, very kind.'

'Yes.'

'I was so afraid when I woke up and realised you'd gone, and walked by yourself all that way. But you did the right thing Tilly.'

'Yes.'

They fell silent, looking at one another. Then Tilly said in a small voice, 'Only I don't think I want to go there for Christmas.'

'But, oh Tilly, no more do I, only we haven't got anything in and I couldn't go shopping – I expect it would be quite grand there but you would have such a dreary time here by yourself with me. I did get you one present but I haven't even managed to wrap it up yet and…'

'But I want it to be just us,' Tilly interrupted, 'here at home. It doesn't matter about presents and things. I know the Kendalls are kind but it wouldn't feel right.'

'No.'

There was the sound of the door, and Miss Kendall's voice calling.

'I'll go,' Tilly said, 'I'll tell her.' She slid off the bed.

If Miss Kendall was either puzzled or offended she certainly didn't show it, she just said that she understood and made Tilly promise that she would telephone them for anything at all that might be needed, and said her mother was not to worry at all about the spoiled dress or the ceiling but only about getting herself completely well again.

'And the nurse will come in twice a day, of course, that's all taken care of,' she said, which Tilly knew meant 'paid for.' Only her mother said that one day she meant to pay the Kendalls back for that because although they had been very generous and kind it was better 'not to be beholden.'

At the end of the afternoon when everyone had finally left, there was a bump at the door and when Tilly opened it, Mr Alec Kendall was standing there, grinning at her over the top of a huge hamper.

'Hang on,' he said 'back in a jiff.'

When he appeared again he was carrying a Christmas tree in a large pot.

'All in order,' he said, winking at her, 'good show.' And he winked at her again and was gone.

Tilly walked round the tree touching the branches here and there. It smelled freshly green and pungent,

as though it were still growing outside. He could put Mrs McBride's ornaments on it and perhaps some scraps of ribbon from her mother's workbox, tied in bows.

Mrs McBride – oh, she must go and see her, she must tell her everything that had happened! But then she remembered that Mrs McBride had gone away – the flat would be empty and dark.

'Christmas,' she said aloud to the little tree. 'Christmas, Christmas, Christmas.'

But the room did not look Christmassy at all and just for a moment she wished she could change her mind and he going to Cliff House where everything would be grand and bright and full of glitter and excitement.

Only she knew in her heart that it would never do, just as she had known it would not do to go Bettina Truman's Boxing Day party, where she would have felt out of place as well, and Bettina's sudden rush of friendliness to her after she had won the doll would have quite faded.

But one day, Tilly thought, standing at the window looking out. One day...

All the same, it was a good Christmas, very, very good, even if everything was somehow upside down and unexpected. The hamper had been stuffed full of treats – things they would never usually have, crystallised fruits and chocolates and pears in brandy, a pineapple and six peaches, mince pies and marzipan animals, a ham and a tongue and a cold roast chicken and even a little flat packet of smoked salmon which her mother said she had not seen since long Beforethewar. There was bottle of sherry and one of port, and a tin of iced biscuits, some crackers and some scented soaps and a decorated candle in a china holder.

And at the very bottom, in a crisp white envelope, there were forty pound notes, to buy a new roll of wedding-dress silk.

Late on Christmas Eve they had a picnic in the bedroom and afterwards Tilly's mother got up for an hour and sat in an armchair and enjoyed the tree, and Mrs McBride's ornaments and Tilly lit the Christmas candle and set it in the window.

As her mother was settling back into bed again she said, 'Oh Tilly, I quite forgot. A parcel was left for you on the door mat. Miss Kendall found it.'

Tilly picked up a familiar cardboard box, tied with green string. It had a note slipped in.

Dear Matilda,

My nephew will deliver this to you as we leave. I wish you both a very happy Christmas and you are to please open this on Christmas Eve, not wait until the morning. It is for you to enjoy this year and then to keep and bring out every Christmas to come, until you are an old, old, white-haired lady like your true friend.

    Christobel McBride.

Tilly turned to her mother and read the letter out loud but then she saw that she was already asleep, settled comfortably on the pillow with her arm curled behind her head. Tilly picked up the box and tiptoed out.

In the living room she turned off the main light and, sitting by the window near the Christmas candle, she opened the box and lifted out the glass tree with its angels and set it on the sill. Then she wound it up very carefully with the tiny gold key in its base. There was a thin gap in the side of the window frame and a faint draught blew in, flickering the flame of the candle, and as the glass angels went round they swung a little and glinted as they caught

the light and touched each other to make a faint
tinkling sound. And, looking out of the window,
Tilly saw that the rain had stopped and the clouds
had parted and that there were stars pricked out in
the clear sky, stars and a thin sliver of moon.

'Oh beautiful!' she said, 'how beautiful.' and sat,
watching the glass angels in the candle-light until she
fell into a half-sleep-half-waking trance, her head on
her arm.

Every year, every single Christmas, she thought,
she would watch the glass angels turning and hear
their music, here in this room and then in other
rooms she had not yet seen, on and on into the far

future, until she was indeed 'an old, old, white-haired lady.' It seemed as if she could see that future, see the pictures of it like the tableaux in the lighted shop windows of the past. The glass angels were a symbol to her of happiness to come, as they had played their part in so many happy Christmases before this one.

One day, Tilly thought. One day…

And for a while she did fall asleep, very lightly, as she sat there.

And was awakened by the first of the midnight bells of Christmas, ringing out across the town.